A Beginning-to-Read Book

Go to Sleep, Dear Dragon

by Margaret Hillert

Illustrated by David Helton

NORWOOD HOUSE PRESS

DEAR CAREGIVER,

The *Beginning-to-Read* series is a carefully written collection of classic readers you may remember from your own childhood. Each book features text comprised of common sight words to provide your child ample practice reading the words that appear most frequently in written text. The many additional details in the pictures enhance the story and offer the opportunity for you to help your child expand oral language and develop comprehension.

Begin by reading the story to your child, followed by letting him or her read familiar words and soon your child will be able to read the story independently. At each step of the way, be sure to praise your reader's efforts to build his or her confidence as an independent reader. Discuss the pictures and encourage your child to make connections between the story and his or her own life. At the end of the story, you will find reading activities and a word list that will help your child practice and strengthen beginning reading skills.

Above all, the most important part of the reading experience is to have fun and enjoy it!

Shannon Cannon

Shannon Cannon,
Literacy Consultant

Norwood House Press • P.O. Box 316598 • Chicago, Illinois 60631
For more information about Norwood House Press please visit our website at *www.norwoodhousepress.com* or call 866-565-2900.

LIBRARY OF CONGRESS CATALOGING-IN-PUBLICATION DATA

Hillert, Margaret.
    Go to sleep, dear dragon / by Margaret Hillert ; illustrated by David Helton.—Rev. and expanded library ed.
        p. cm. — (Beginning to read series. Dear dragon)
    Summary: After reading a book about medieval times, a boy falls asleep and dreams that he is in a medieval setting where he finds a big egg out of which a baby dragon hatches. Includes reading activities.
    ISBN-13: 978-1-59953-018-5 (library edition : alk. paper)
    ISBN-10: 1-59953-018-X (library edition : alk. paper)
    [1. Dragons—Fiction. 2. Dreams--Fiction. 3. Readers.] I. Helton, David, ill. II. Title. III. Series.
    PZ7.H558Go 2006
    [E]—dc22   2005033516

Go to sleep, dear dragon.
Go to sleep.
This is a good thing for
us to do.

Oh, what is this?
What do I see here?
Where am I?

How did I get here?
What is this spot?
Where is my house?

Look here.
Look here.
How big this one is!
It is not my house.

I will go in.
I will go in to see
what I can see.

Oh, my. Oh, my.
What have we here?
It looks like fun.

I see this.
I see that.
I can look and
look and look.

Look at this man.
See what he can do.
He is good.

And look here.
One, two, three.
One is down.
Two are up, up, up.

And what is this?
What do I see now?

One man is up.
One man is down.

He is good.
He will get something.
Something pretty.

Here is a pretty little one.
It can run and jump.
I like this one.

What fun this is!

But I have to go now.
Mother and Father will
want me.
I will go to my house.

That is funny.
I see something,
but what is it?
I can't make
it out.

And what do I see here?
Here is something big.
Big, big, big.

I guess no one wants it.
No one is here.
No one can see it but me.

Now, what is this?
Look here. Look here.
Look at this.
Something will come out.

CRACK!

Oh, my! Oh, my!
A baby dragon.
A little baby dragon.

Oh, how little you are!
But you will get big.

You can play with me.
We can have fun.

Come to my house.
I like you.
I want you with me.
I will find something
good for you to eat.

Here you are with me.
And here I am with you.
Oh, what a happy dream,
dear dragon.

READING REINFORCEMENT

The following activities support the findings of the National Reading Panel that determined the most effective components for reading instruction are: Phonemic Awareness, Phonics, Vocabulary, Fluency, and Text Comprehension.

Phonemic Awareness: The /sl/ sound

Oddity Task: Say the /**sl**/ sound for your child. Ask your child to say the word that doesn't begin with the /**sl**/ sound in the following word groups:

ship, slip, sleep	sled, sad, slide	slick, sling, spot
sat, slim, sled,	slice, sign, sleeve	slate, see, sliver
slow, slug, shake	something, slant, slipper	

Phonics: The letter Kk

1. Demonstrate how to form the letters **K** and **k** for your child.

2. Have your child practice writing **K** and **k** at least three times each.

3. Ask your child to point to the words in the book that have the letter **k** in them.

4. Explain to your child that when the letter **k** is followed by the letter **n** it is silent—doesn't make a sound.

5. Write the words listed below and ask your child to point to them and repeat them.

know	knight	knock	knit	knee
knob	knife	knuckle	knot	knead

6. Say the words in random order and ask your child to point to the right word.

7. Ask your child to read the words he or she can from the list.

Vocabulary: Story Words

1. Write the following words on separate pieces of paper and point to them as you read them to your child:

castle   dragon   jester   knight   princess

2. Say the following sentences aloud and ask your child to point to the word that is described:

- Once upon a time there was a big, beautiful place where the king and queen lived. (castle)
- The man on the horse who had shiny armor was called a (knight).
- The daughter of the king and queen was called a (princess).
- What hatched out of the egg that the boy found in his dream? (dragon)
- The funny man who juggled the balls in the air is called a what? (jester)

Fluency: Echo Reading

1. Reread the story to your child at least two more times while your child tracks the print by running a finger under the words as they are read. Ask your child to read the words he or she knows with you.

2. Reread the story, stopping after each sentence or page to allow your child to read (echo) what you have read. Repeat echo reading and let your child take the lead.

Text Comprehension: Discussion Time

1. Ask your child to retell the sequence of events in the story.

2. To check comprehension, ask your child the following questions:

- Why do you think the words and pictures in this story are in bubbles? (to help the reader understand that the boy is dreaming)
- If you lived during the time of the dream, which character would you like to be? Why?

WORD LIST

***Go to Sleep, Dear Dragon* uses the 74 words listed below.**
This list can be used to practice reading the words that appear in the text. You may wish to write the words on index cards and use them to help your child build automatic word recognition. Regular practice with these words will enhance your child's fluency in reading connected text.

a	eat	I	oh	up
am		in	one	us
and	Father	is	out	
are	find	it		want
at	for		play	we
	fun	jump	pretty	what
baby	funny			where
big		like	run	will
but	get	little		with
	go	look	see	
can	good		sleep	you
can't	guess	make	something	
come		man	spot	
	happy	me		
did	have	Mother	that	
dear	he	my	thing	
do	here		this	
dragon	house	no	three	
dream	how	not	to	
down		now	two	

ABOUT THE AUTHOR Margaret Hillert has written over 80 books for children who are just learning to read. Her books have been translated into many different languages and over a million children throughout the world have read her books. She first started writing poetry as a child and has continued to write for children and adults throughout her life. A first grade teacher for 34 years, Margaret is now retired from teaching and lives in Michigan where she likes to write, take walks in the morning, and care for her three cats.

Photograph by Glenna Washburn

ABOUT THE ADVISER Shannon Cannon contributed the activities pages that appear in this book. Shannon serves as a literacy consultant and provides staff development to help improve reading instruction. She is a frequent presenter at educational conferences and workshops. Prior to this she worked as an elementary school teacher and as president of a curriculum publishing company.